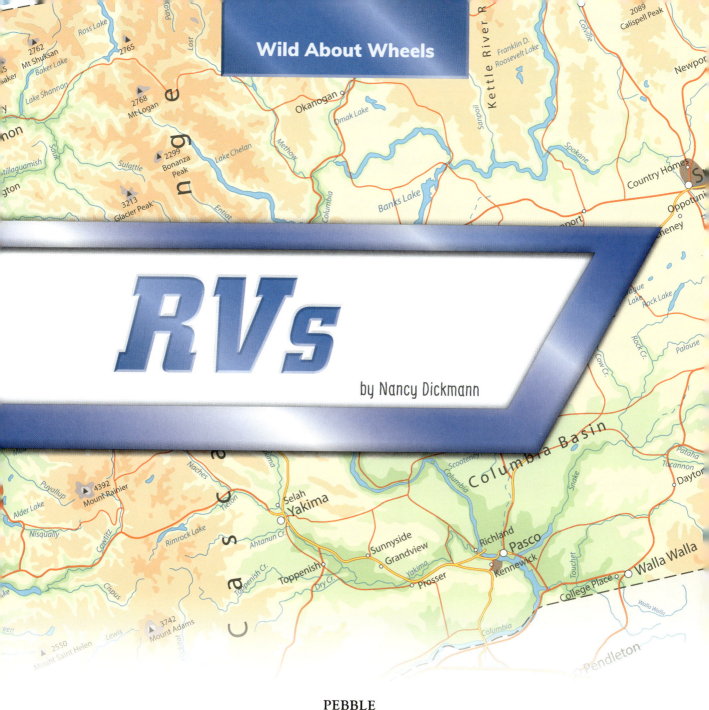

Wild About Wheels

RVs

by Nancy Dickmann

PEBBLE
a capstone imprint

Pebble Emerge is published by Pebble, an imprint of Capstone.
1710 Roe Crest Drive
North Mankato, Minnesota 56003
www.capstonepub.com

Copyright © 2021 by Capstone. All rights reserved. No part of this publication may be reproduced in whole or in part, or stored in a retrieval system, or transmitted in any form or by any means, electronic, mechanical, photocopying, recording, or otherwise, without written permission of the publisher.

Library of Congress Cataloging-in-Publication Data is available on the Library of Congress website.
ISBN: 978-1-9771-2481-4 (hardcover)
ISBN: 978-1-9771-2523-1 (eBook PDF)

Summary: Describes recreational vehicles, including the different types of RVs, their main parts, and how people use them.

Image Credits
Capstone Studio: Karon Dubke, 21; Dreamstime: Bounder32h, 14–15; Getty Images: Yellow Dog Productions, 6; iStockphoto: Arnaud-h, 8, IPGGutenbergUKLtd, 4, JaySi, 10, jstephens33, 17, olrat, 12; Shutterstock: AnjelikaGr, 11, Arina P Habich, 18–19, Cartarium, background (map), Greg and Jan Ritchie, 5, Ilona Koeleman, 13, Robert Paul Van Beets, 9, Stuart Perry, 7, Tupun-gato, cover, back cover; SuperStock: fStop Images, 16

Editorial Credits
Editor: Carrie Sheely; Designer: Cynthia Della-Rovere; Media Researcher: Eric Gohl; Production Specialist: Katy LaVigne

All internet sites appearing in back matter were available and accurate when this book was sent to press.

Printed and bound in the USA.
003422

Table of Contents

What RVs Do 4

Look Inside. 8

Look Outside. 14

RV Diagram 18

Design Your Own RV 20

Glossary 22

Read More 23

Internet Sites 23

Index 24

Words in **bold** are in the glossary.

What RVs Do

It's time to go camping! It's fun to spend time away from home. Will you camp in the woods? Maybe you will go to a park.

An RV makes camping easy. It is like a home on wheels you can take with you. RV is short for recreational **vehicle**. Sometimes people call RVs campers.

Some RVs have **engines**. An engine powers the RV. The driver sits in the front. Some RVs are not driven. Other vehicles pull them.

Some RVs are as big as a bus. Some are small. But that doesn't mean they feel crowded! The roof might pop up. The sides might slide out. This makes more space.

Look Inside

You're tired! Go to your bed. Many RVs have one bed on the floor. A different bed is placed right over it. These are bunk beds.

bunk beds

It's time to wake up! Where can you get ready for the day? Most RVs have a bathroom. It has a sink, mirror, and toilet. There might be a small shower too.

Time for lunch! It's easy to cook in an RV. There is a fridge. There is a stove. There might be an oven. When it's time to clean up, you can wash dishes in the kitchen sink.

RVs have other things that you would find at home. They have tables and chairs. They have sofas to sit on. You can put clothes, toys, and books in drawers.

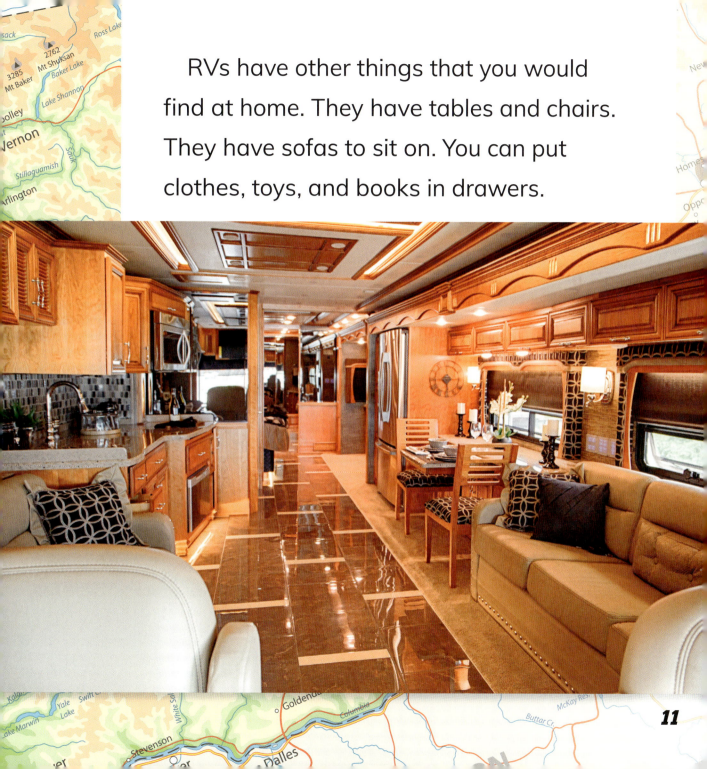

Most RVs use **electricity**. Electricity powers the lights and machines to make them work. An RV can plug into an electrical outlet to use electricity.

Electricity can also come from a **battery**. A battery stores **energy**. It can use the energy to make electricity. Then the RV doesn't need to be plugged in.

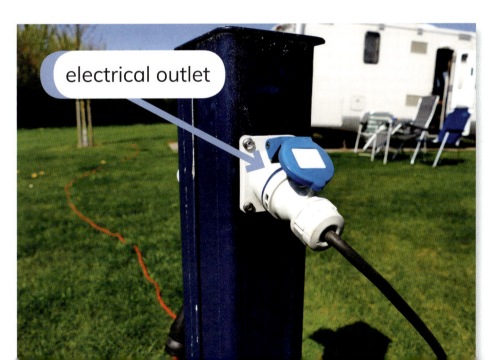

electrical outlet

Look Outside

Many RVs look alike from the outside. Many are shaped like rectangles. But some small campers are shaped like teardrops. Some have pointed or rounded fronts.

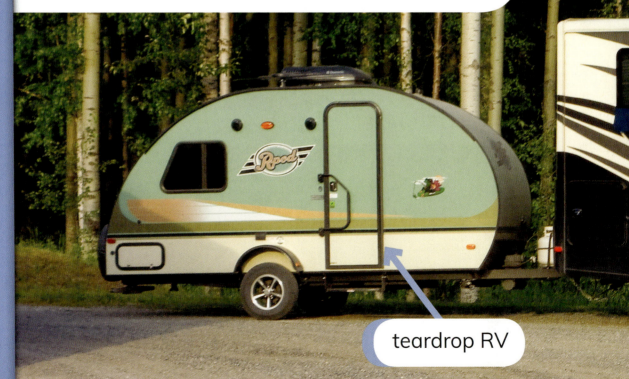

teardrop RV

How many wheels does an RV have? The bigger the RV is, the more wheels it usually has. Really big ones might have six. Some small ones that are pulled have two.

Camping and the outdoors go together. RVs have windows to look outside. Most have an **awning**. It can stretch out. People can sit under it to get out of the hot sun.

Some RVs have body parts that fold up or out. What's inside? It might be an outdoor kitchen or a TV!

awning

RV Diagram

slide-out body part

Design Your Own RV

If you could design an RV, what would it look like? Will it be pulled or driven? How many rooms will it have? Will it have bunk beds to save space? What will the kitchen look like? Draw your RV on the outside. Then draw a plan of the inside.

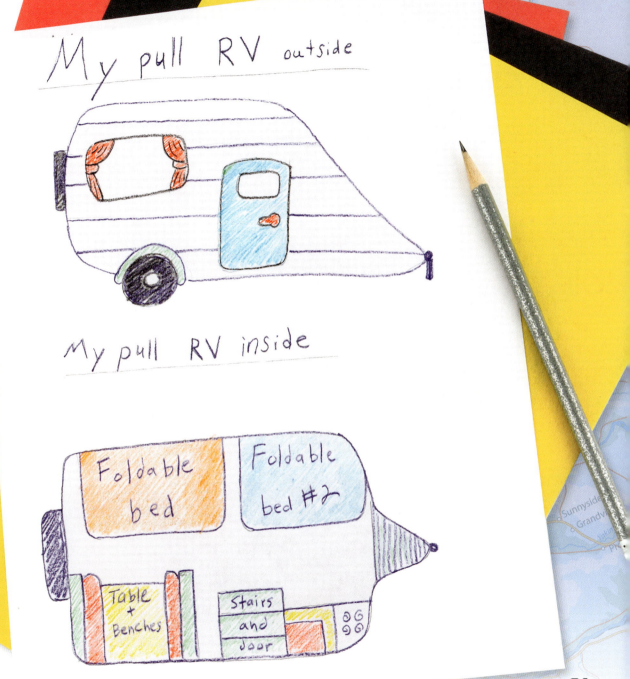

Glossary

awning (AWN-ing)—a cover that can stretch out from the side of an RV

battery (BA-tuh-ree)—a container that stores energy; a battery can produce electricity

electricity (i-lek-TRISS-uh-tee)—energy made by the flow of charged particles

energy (EN-ur-jee)—the ability to do work

engine (EN-juhn)—a machine that uses fuel to power a vehicle

vehicle (VEE-uh-kuhl)—a machine used to carry people or things, such as a car or truck

Read More

Erin, McHugh. *National Parks: A Kid's Guide to America's Parks, Monuments, and Landmarks.* New York: Black Dog & Leventhal, 2019.

Meister, Cari. *Trucks.* North Mankato, MN: Capstone, 2019.

Internet Sites

Go RVing: RV History
https://gorving.com/discover-rving/rv-history

JPkid.com
https://www.jpkid.com

Index

awnings, 16

bathrooms, 9
batteries, 13
beds, 8

chairs, 11
cooking, 10

drawers, 11
drivers, 6

electricity, 13
engines, 6

fridges, 10

kitchens, 10, 16

ovens, 10

showers, 9
sinks, 9, 10
stoves, 10

tables, 11
toilets, 9

wheels, 4, 15